YOU ARE MY SUNSHINE

Retold by BLAKE HOENA

Illustrated by KIM BARNES

CANTATA
LEARNING

WWW.CANTATALEARNING.COM

**CANTATA
LEARNING**

Published by Cantata Learning
1710 Roe Crest Drive
North Mankato, MN 56003
www.cantatalearning.com

Library of Congress Control Number: 2015932822
Hoena, Blake
    You Are My Sunshine / retold by Blake Hoena; Illustrated by Kim Barnes
    Series: Tangled Tunes
    Audience: Ages: 3–8; Grades: PreK–3
    Summary: In this twist on the classic song "You Are My Sunshine," a little girl
learns about the rising and setting of the bright, warm sun and all of the good
things it does to brighten her day.
    ISBN: 978-1-63290-368-6 (library binding/CD)
    ISBN: 978-1-63290-499-7 (paperback/CD)
    ISBN: 978-1-63290-529-1 (paperback)
    1. Stories in rhyme. 2. Sun—fiction. 3. Weather—fiction.

Book design and art direction, Tim Palin Creative
Editorial direction, Flat Sole Studio
Music direction, Elizabeth Draper
Music arranged and produced by Musical Youth Productions

Printed in the United States of America in North Mankato, Minnesota.
122015   0326CGS16

Without the sun, Earth would be a cold, dark place. **Sunshine** brings us light and **warmth**. It helps plants grow and brightens our days.

Now turn the page and sing along to learn more about our big, bright sun!

You are my sunshine,
my only sunshine.

You make me happy
with your bright **rays**.

You rise in the east
to start the day.

Please don't take my sunshine away.

You are my sunshine,
my only sunshine.

You make me happy
with your bright rays.

The clouds rolled in.

The sky turned gray.

Please don't take my sunshine away.

You are my sunshine,
my only sunshine.

You make me happy
with your bright rays.

I think about you
on rainy days.

Please don't take my sunshine away.

When I looked out my bedroom window
it was sunny, with no more gray.

Across the sky stretched a rainbow,
so I went outside to play.

You are my sunshine,
my only sunshine.

You make me happy
with your bright rays.

You make the trees grow
and flowers **bloom**.

Please don't take my sunshine away.

You are my sunshine,
my only sunshine.

You make me happy
with your bright rays.

You set in the west
to end the day.

Please don't take my sunshine away.

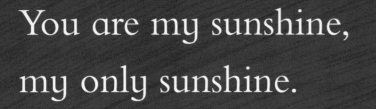

You are my sunshine,
my only sunshine.

You make me happy
with your bright rays.

I think about you
when I am dreaming.

Oh, I hope you come back some day.

SONG LYRICS
You Are My Sunshine

You are my sunshine,
my only sunshine.

You make me happy
with your bright rays.

You rise in the east
to start the day.

Please don't take my sunshine away.

You are my sunshine,
my only sunshine.

You make me happy
with your bright rays.

The clouds rolled in.
The sky turned gray.

Please don't take my sunshine away.

You are my sunshine,
my only sunshine.

You make me happy
with your bright rays.

I think about you
on rainy days.

Please don't take my sunshine away.

When I looked out my bedroom
    window
it was sunny, with no more gray.

Across the sky stretched a rainbow,
so I went outside to play.

You are my sunshine,
my only sunshine.

You make me happy
with your bright rays.

You make the trees grow
and flowers bloom.

Please don't take my sunshine away.

You are my sunshine,
my only sunshine.

You make me happy
with your bright rays.

You set in the west
to end the day.

Please don't take my sunshine away.

You are my sunshine,
my only sunshine.

You make me happy
with your bright rays.

I think about you
when I am dreaming.

Oh, I hope you come back
    some day.

You Are My Sunshine

Zydeco/Pop
Musical Youth Productions

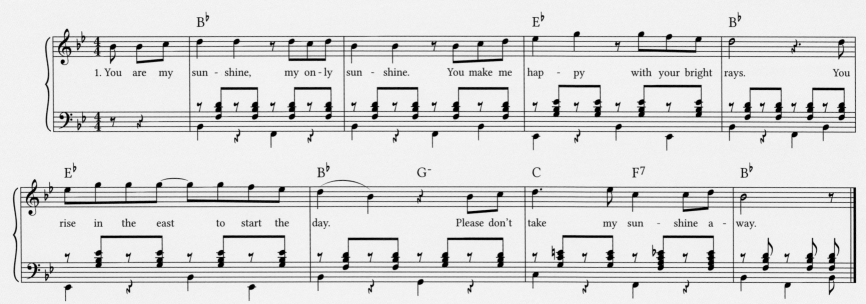

1. You are my sun - shine, my on - ly sun - shine. You make me hap - py with your bright rays. You rise in the east to start the day. Please don't take my sun - shine a - way.

Verse 2
You are my sunshine,
my only sunshine.
You make me happy
with your bright rays.

The clouds rolled in.
The sky turned gray.
Please don't take my sunshine away.

Verse 3
You are my sunshine,
my only sunshine.
You make me happy
with your bright rays.

I think about you
on rainy days.
Please don't take my sunshine away.

Verse 4
When I looked out
my bedroom window
it was sunny,
with no more gray.

Across the sky
stretched a rainbow,
so I went outside to play.

Verse 5
You are my sunshine,
my only sunshine.
You make me happy
with your bright rays.

You make the trees grow
and flowers bloom.
Please don't take my sunshine away.

Verse 6
You are my sunshine,
my only sunshine.
You make me happy
with your bright rays.

You set in the west
to end the day.
Please don't take my sunshine away.

Verse 7
You are my sunshine,
my only sunshine.
You make me happy
with your bright rays.

I think about you
when I am dreaming.
Oh, I hope you come back some day.

GLOSSARY

bloom—to make flowers

rays—lines of light

sunshine—the sun's light

warmth—the state of being warm

GUIDED READING ACTIVITIES

1. When does the sun rise during the day? When does it set?

2. The sunshine makes the girl in this story happy. What makes you happy?

3. What was the weather like today? Was it sunny? Rainy? Cloudy? Snowy? Draw a picture of today's weather.

TO LEARN MORE

Boothroyd, Jennifer. *What Does Sunlight Do?* Minneapolis: Lerner, 2014.

Cannons, Helen Cox. *Sunshine*. North Mankato, MN: Heinemann-Raintree, 2015.

Davis, Jimmie. *You Are My Sunshine*. New York: Cartwheel Books, 2011.

Ghigna, Charles. *Sunshine Brightens Springtime*. North Mankato, MN: Picture Window Books, 2015.